A Beginning-to-Read Book

# Who Feels Happy, Dear Dragon?

by Margaret Hillert

Illustrated by Jack Pullan

NORWOOD HOUSE PRESS

**DEAR CAREGIVER,** The *Beginning-to-Read* series is comprised of carefully written books that extend the collection of classic readers you may remember from your own childhood. Each book features text comprised of common sight words to provide your child ample practice reading the words that appear most frequently in written text. The many additional details in the pictures enhance the story and offer the opportunity for you to help your child expand oral language and develop comprehension.

Begin by reading the story to your child, followed by letting him or her read familiar words and soon your child will be able to read the story independently. At each step of the way, be sure to praise your reader's efforts to build his or her confidence as an independent reader. Discuss the pictures and encourage your child to make connections between the story and his or her own life. At the end of the story, you will find reading activities and a word list that will help your child practice and strengthen beginning reading skills.

Above all, the most important part of the reading experience is to have fun and enjoy it!

*Shannon Cannon*

Shannon Cannon, Ph.D., Literacy Consultant

Norwood House Press • P.O. Box 316598 • Chicago, Illinois 60631
For more information about Norwood House Press please visit our website at
*www.norwoodhousepress.com* or call 866-565-2900.

**LIBRARY OF CONGRESS CATALOGING-IN-PUBLICATION DATA**
Names: Hillert, Margaret, author. | Pullan, Jack, illustrator.
Title: Who feels happy, Dear Dragon? / by Margaret Hillert ; illustrated by
   Jack Pullan.
Description: Chicago, IL : Norwood House Press, [2017] | Series: A
   beginning-to-read book | Summary: "A boy and his pet dragon enjoy
   activities that make them feel happy including; making new friends, and
   getting a new pet kitten. This title includes reading activities and a
   word list"-- Provided by publisher.
Identifiers: LCCN 2016052217 (print) | LCCN 2017014184 (ebook) | ISBN
   9781684040070 (eBook) | ISBN 9781599538242 (library edition : alk. paper)
Subjects: | CYAC: Happiness--Fiction. | Cats--Fiction. |
   Animals--Infancy--Fiction. | Dragons--Fiction.
Classification: LCC PZ7.H558 (ebook) | LCC PZ7.H558 Wgt 2017 (print) | DDC
   [E]--dc23
LC record available at https://lccn.loc.gov/2016052217

Hardcover ISBN: 978-1-59953-824-2          Paperback ISBN: 978-1-68404-002-5

302N–072017
Manufactured in the United States of America in North Mankato, Minnesota.

Oh Mother come in here and look.

Look how pretty they are.

4

One is yellow.
One is black and white.
One looks like a tiger.

Please can I have this one?
I will take good care of it.

Yes, but will Spot like it?

Yes the dog likes the kitten.
We can keep this kitten.

The kitten will need this
—and this
—and this.

Thank you! Thank you!
I am so happy.
We will call the kitten Happy!

I will go out and play now.

I am up.
You are down.
I am happy when we play.

Look over there.
I want to play!

Can I play too?
This looks fun!

Yes!
It is fun to play!
Here.

Go out there.
I will hit the ball.
Look for the ball.

Ready?
Here it comes!
Go! Go! Go!

I got the ball!
I did it!

This was fun.
I am happy with my new friends!

I like to play.
But we should go home and eat.

Run! Run!
Let's go see Happy the cat.

I am home Mother!
What a good day.
I am so happy!

We got a kitten.
We played in the park.
We made friends.
Now we can eat something good!

Here you are with me.
And here I am with you.
Oh what a happy day, Dear Dragon.

# READING REINFORCEMENT

The following activities support the findings of the National Reading Panel that determined the most effective components for reading instruction are: Phonemic Awareness, Phonics, Vocabulary, Fluency, and Text Comprehension.

## Phonemic Awareness: The /h/ sound

**Sound Substitution:** Say the words on the left to your child. Ask your child to repeat the word, changing the first sound to /**h**/:

| | | |
|---|---|---|
| good = hood | look = hook | bit = hit |
| sat = hat | call = hall | be = he |
| like = hike | now = how | will = hill |

## Phonics: The letter Hh

1. Demonstrate how to form the letters **H** and **h** for your child.

2. Have your child practice writing **H** and **h** at least three times each.

3. Ask your child to point to the words in the book that begin with the letter **h**.

4. Write down the following words and ask your child to write the letter **h** in front of them to make a new word:

   | | | | |
   |---|---|---|---|
   | _am | _and | _ill | _at |
   | _all | _air | _ear | _ow |

5. Read the words aloud. Ask your child to read all the words he or she knows.

## Vocabulary: Story Words

1. Write the following words on separate pieces of paper and point to them as you read them to your child:

   | | | | |
   |---|---|---|---|
   | kitten | ball | run | happy |
   | eat | park | dog | play |

2. Say the following sentences aloud and ask your child to point to the word that is described:

- A baby cat is also called a (kitten).
- In baseball, you hit the (ball) with a bat.
- When you want to get somewhere fast, you (run).
- How you feel when things are good. (happy).
- You (eat) when you are hungry.
- It is fun to go to the (park) to play with friends.
- An animal you can have as a pet. (dog)
- You can (play) a game with your friends.

## Fluency: Shared Reading

1. Reread the story to your child at least two more times while your child tracks the print by running a finger under the words as they are read. Ask your child to read the words he or she knows with you.

2. Reread the story taking turns, alternating readers between sentences or pages.

## Text Comprehension: Discussion Time

1. Ask your child to retell the sequence of events in the story.

2. To check comprehension, ask your child the following questions:

- What did the boy name his pet kitten?
- Does Spot like Happy?
- What sport do the boy and Dear Dragon play with friends?
- How did the boy feel at the end of the day after getting a kitten, playing in the park, and making new friends?
- What is something that makes you feel happy? Why?

## WORD LIST

***Who Feels Happy, Dear Dragon?* uses the 85 words listed below.**

The **4** words bolded below serve as an introduction to new vocabulary, while the other 81 are pre-primer. You may wish to write the words on index cards and use them to help your child build automatic word recognition. Regular practice with these words will enhance your child's fluency in reading connected text.

| | | | | | |
|---|---|---|---|---|---|
| a | eat | I | of | take | want |
| am | | in | oh | thank | was |
| and | for | is | one | the | we |
| are | **friends** | it | out | there | what |
| | fun | | over | they | when |
| ball | | keep | | this | white |
| black | go | **kitten** | **park** | **tiger** | will |
| but | good | | play | to | with |
| | got | lets | played | too | |
| call | | like (s) | please | | yellow |
| can | happy | look (s) | pretty | up | yes |
| care | have | | | | you |
| cat | here | made | ready | | |
| come (s) | hit | me | run | | |
| | home | mother | | | |
| day | how | my | see | | |
| dear | | | should | | |
| did | | need | so | | |
| dog | | new | something | | |
| down | | now | Spot | | |
| dragon | | | | | |

**ABOUT THE AUTHOR** Margaret Hillert has helped millions of children all over the world learn to read independently. She was a first grade teacher for 34 years and during that time started writing books that her students could both gain confidence in reading and enjoy. She wrote well over 100 books for children just learning to read. As a child, she enjoyed writing poetry and continued her poetic writings as an adult for both children and adults.

*Photograph by Glenna Washburn*

**ABOUT THE ILLUSTRATOR** A talented and creative illustrator, Jack Pullan, is a graduate of William Jewell College. He has also studied informally at Oxford University and the Kansas City Art Institute. He was mentored by the renowned watercolor artists, Jim Hamil and Bill Amend. Jack's work has graced the pages of many enjoyable children's books, various educational materials, cartoon strips, as well as many greeting cards. Jack currently resides in Kansas.